TREE NINJA'S

A Children's Tale

Written and illustrated by a very clever Ben Hayford A.K.A Tree Ninja

Welcome to the world of the Tree Ninjas!

Are they good at their job? Sometimes...
Are they clever? Thats debatable...
Do they have the necessary skills to make this book more interesting? Oh yes they do!

Join Ben, Jack, Martina, and whole group of hard working equipment on their journey through everyday life in the world of tree surgery.

The stories told in this book are based loosely on a real tree surgery company run by a man called Ben (me).
I have had the amazing pleasure of working with some brilliant characters over the years, which are brought to life inside.

Will it make you become a tree surgeon? Probably not.
Will it make you laugh? ummm, 1000%!!
Enjoy!

It was a lovely sunny morning at the Tree Ninja's house, and everybody was asleep. But then...

Quick, Lets go!!

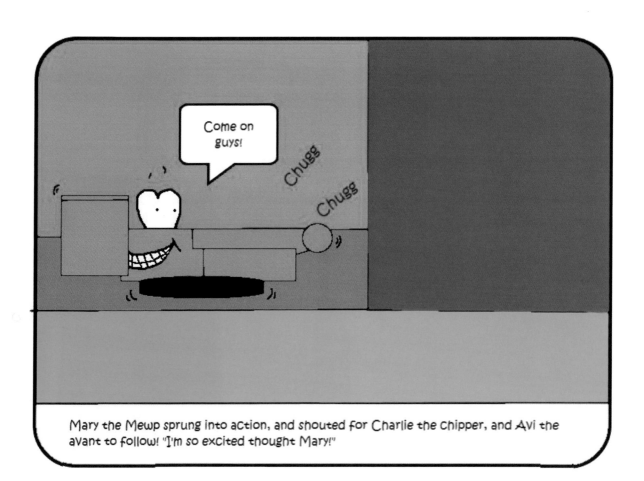

Mary the Mewp sprung into action, and shouted for Charlie the Chipper, and Avi the avant to follow! "I'm so excited thought Mary!"

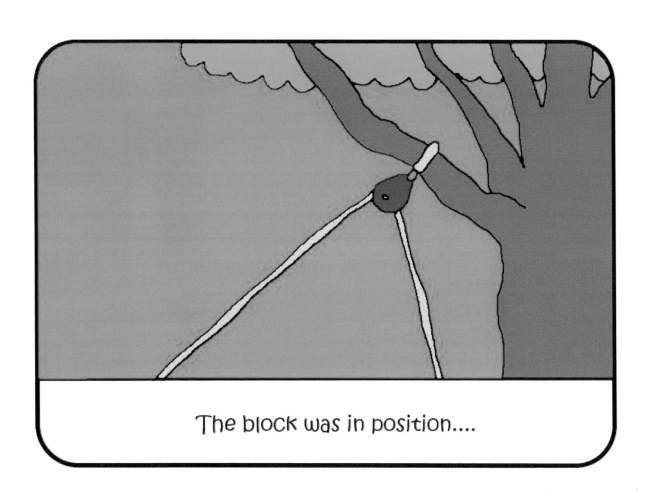

The block was in position....

Ben used Mary to attach the rope...

The tree started to lift up off the house!

Snap!

'OH NO!' said Ben

The house was destroyed!!

Oh dear. Things just got abit worse....

The Ninjas became trapped!

Avi lifts the huge tree with his grab Claws...

Now the Ninjas were free, they started to cut up the large tree.

The last log was being loaded. Now it was Charlies turn...

But did Ben really have an idea??..

'What's your idea Ben?' Said Jack.
'Lets close our eyes' Ben said. 'When we are asleep we can pretend today never happened....'

TREE NINJA'S

The one hour job.

'Hi Ben' Said Jack. 'What job do we have on today?'

Luckily Ben and Jack were very quick, and very skilled....

The branches were falling so fast Jack, and
Charlie struggled to keep up!

'How far shall we move back?' asked Charlie the Chipper.
'How far is our house?' replied Jack.

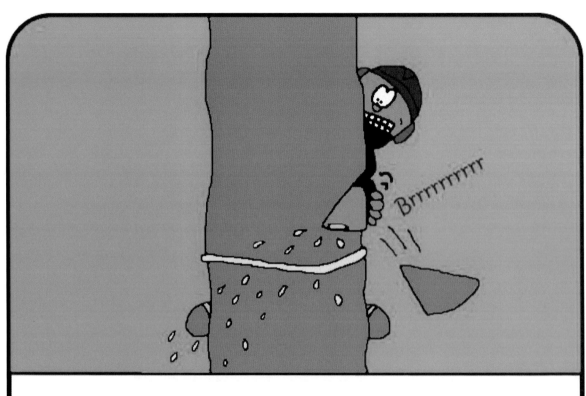

With dinner ready in 10 minutes Ben did not think about exactly how big the top of the tree was.....

With the top of the tree in the clouds, this was going to make a very large bang when it hits the ground....

Just as Ben made the final cut, he realised just how big the top was!

The hole in the grass was so deep, Ben wondered
if it reached the other side of the earth!

'How are we going to get the tree out of that hole?? said Jack.

Before Jack, and Charlie the Chipper realised, Ben had come down from the tree, and was shouting 'Timber!'

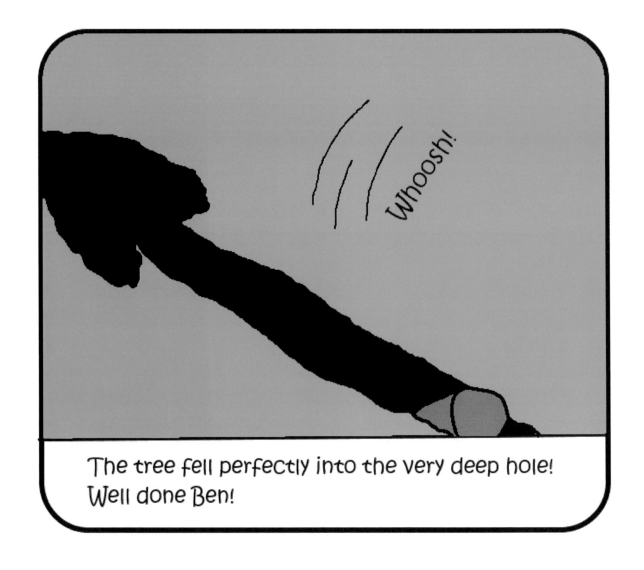

The tree fell perfectly into the very deep hole!
Well done Ben!

With the whole tree now in the hole Jack had a question..

Oh dear. Ben has another idea......

Ben was interupted by a loud scream!!!

All of a sudden Ben's legs started moving and would not stop....

Ben made it home safe, and in perfect time for dinner!

As Ben laid in his comfortable bed after eating his amazing dinner. He suddenly realised that Jack, and Charley the Chipper had not returned! But where were they??...............

"Jack please get out of the hole!" said Charley the Chipper. "Im really tired"

The End.

'Thankyou for reading me.... you are the best!'

Printed in Great Britain
by Amazon

80828154R00031